I0618295

THOUGHT CATALOG BOOKS

Good Night's Sleep

Good Night's Sleep

JACK FOLLMAN

Thought Catalog Books

Brooklyn, NY

THOUGHT CATALOG BOOKS

Copyright © 2016 by The Thought & Expression Co.

All rights reserved. Published by Thought Catalog Books, a division of The Thought & Expression Co., Williamsburg, Brooklyn. Founded in 2010, Thought Catalog is a website and imprint dedicated to your ideas and stories. We publish fiction and non-fiction from emerging and established writers across all genres. For general information and submissions: manuscripts@thoughtcatalog.com.

First edition, 2016

ISBN 978-0692666050

10 9 8 7 6 5 4 3 2 1

Cover photography by © jarino47

Contents

1

A Few Years Before

I found a note, a poem really, tucked into the door of my car today. I don't think it was for me though. Scrawled on a standard piece of notepaper, wilted by the light rain of the day.

I read it aloud to myself in my car as I listened to that same rain trickle on the roof of my car.

It's okay to be a ghost. It has its pleasures. You're light. You float. You slip in and out unseen. There's no love to lose or burden to be. You have so little to hold you down. You are free.

Some pearls are never found. They hide under the sand on the ocean floor. No one knows they're there. But the pearl knows. Maybe there was a time he wanted to be found. To be seen. And to be held. But now, only hope hurts. I am my own secret. A secret kept by me.

Something has changed. Now the ghost is scared. He cannot float. He's heavy. He's flesh and blood. He must open doors. He can't slip away unseen. The ghost is sad. All those years invisible haunt him now. Why didn't he try? Or care? Or be?

The ghost is happy. He is found. He is held. And he is seen.

The ghost is seen.

I crumpled up the poem without much thought, threw it away in the trash in my kitchen.

It wasn't for me.

2

November

Unfortunately sleep apnea runs in my family. I remember family vacations where I considered cashing in all of my allowance money so I could get my own hotel room and not have to listen to the epic snoring battle taking place between my parents in the bed next to me. The two sounded like the tragically stupid boys from my middle school years who would sit outside on the benches at lunch trying to see who could hock the biggest loogies upon the hot concrete being played on repeat.

I had made it 29 years in life without ever being accused of snoring by any former roommates, boyfriends or family. However, a few months of regularly waking up feeling out of breath with my heart racing coupled with a healthy dose of click bait websites discussing sleep apnea convinced me the dark Petersen family curse had finally descended upon me. I went to the doctor with visions of scaring away every potential future mate by wearing a sleep apnea mask which made me look like some kind of H.R. Giger nightmare and sound like Darth Vader.

I was not diagnosed yet, though. My HMO-financed physician who had a rickety office above a dry cleaner in a part of town that had never even heard of the word "gentrification" told me the cheapest way to figure out if I had sleep apnea or not would be to simply record myself sleeping each night for a few weeks. He would review the tapes when I turned them in and let me know if I had it.

I thoroughly questioned the method, but my doctor explained the other option of coming into a facility to do extensive testing would cost upwards of $2,000, even with my wonderful insurance. It would also require me to sleep in a doctor's office a few times which actually sounded worse than giving my physician a free voyeur video. Still, I was going to pass on doing it before one of his nurses mentioned to me she did the same exact method herself and it had been fine. The presence of a wedding band on her finger and a child growing visibly growing inside of her stomach convinced me to trust her. I figured you have to be trustworthy enough to get married and pregnant. One or the other might be a different story, but both, that's good enough for me.

I couldn't help but laugh that night when I set up my camera and tripod aimed at my bed like I was going to shoot some kind of low-budget porn, but I figured it was worth it to find out if I had an ailment that would shave years off of my life and to save some serious money. I couldn't help but regret spending the amount I had on music festivals and happy hours the past calendar year and how saving that money would have probably allowed me to do the testing in a normal manner. Fuck it, I probably would have just spent it on something stupid anyway.

The biggest down side of the thing to me was I had to wear pajamas for the first time since I was a preteen. I had grown accustomed to sleeping in my birthday suit to help in keeping myself cool in the fight against the warm Southern

California nights and now I was going to be sweating in my striped cotton get up that made me feel like I should have been a parent in a wholesome 50s sitcom.

The three weeks of filming went by quickly. I was putting in long days at work, just stumbling home at 11 and crashing each night. The only time the filming actually really affected me was one Saturday when I came home drunk, hit record and passed out fully clothed on top of the covers. I considered deleting my drunken moment but figured it might actually be good to have a comparison to see how getting piss drunk affected my potential sleep apnea.

It took about a month before I was summoned back to my doctor's office to go over the results.

Things started out well. My doctor told me he didn't think I had sleep apnea and I had saved thousands of dollars and countless hours of facility testing.

But things quickly took a sharp turn.

I still remember my doctor casually saying the phrase that completely changed my life.

"The only time I really noticed even minor disturbances in your sleep pattern was when your boyfriend would come in and out of the bed."

My heart dropped to my stomach. My face burned. I swallowed before I spoke.

"I don't have a boyfriend."

I wondered at first if the doctor had the wrong video, but once he popped in my familiar flash drive and showed me collapse into my bed I knew he had been watching the right video. I saw myself lying alone in my bed, but after about a minute of watching me sleep in fast forward I saw what he was talking about.

An hour into the first night of my recorded slumber a male figure appeared in the field of vision of the camera. Tall, gaunt, dressed in black with a head of long black hair that obscured his face, I couldn't get a real read on exactly how the man looked, but he appeared to be white and probably in his 20s or 30s. I felt bile bubble up to the back of my throat when I watched him stealthily slide on top of the covers on the side of my king size bed I didn't sleep on, fold his arms across his chest and just lie there, staring up at the ceiling.

"What the fuck?" I said and recoiled into my plastic chair. "How did I never wake up?"

"Well, I have to say you are the deepest sleeper I have ever reviewed," my doctor assured me just before I vomited all over myself.

I cleaned myself up and watched all of the nights I recorded myself in the doctor's office. Each night followed the same routine: I would go to sleep and an hour or so later, the man, who never gave the camera a good look at his face, entered, laid down next to me and then left just before sunrise. The man never did anything sinister, never anything sexual, never even touched me and for some reason it made the whole thing much worse.

The cops were little to no help. Weaned on a steady diet of cop shows, I expected to be helped out by a dangerously-attractive male/female duo of detectives in their late-20s/

early-30s who regularly peppered their conversation with flirtations. Instead, I got one middle-aged guy with ears caked with flaky psoriasis who all but admitted he didn't give a shit about my case. He directly mentioned that any case without violence took a backseat in a district which was home to gangs of five different ethnicities.

Every night after that day was been outright hell. I didn't even go back to my apartment. I had my dad go in there and get my important shit and moved into my old room at my parents' house, 15 miles away from my old apartment.

Despite my parents' high-tech security system, heavy locks on my old bedroom door and windows, the presence of my former USC linebacker dad in the house and the family German Shepherd sleeping outside my door, I would be lucky if I could muster a few hours of restless sleep each night. Everything in my life suffered. I could hardly focus at work, my already-struggling social life became non-existent and I had zero trust for any male I met, so forget about dating.

Things got so bad I eventually decided the best idea would be to just move from my hometown of LA where I had lived in for my entire life. Work was happy to offer me a position in their Atlanta headquarters to try and rejuvenate my life capabilities. So, after six months of persisting torture, I packed up my stuff and headed across the country to move in with my cousin Felicia who was hell bent on turning my life around.

Things got better in Atlanta. The anonymity it brought to my life and the distance it gave me from the incident slowly brought me back to life.

The cops in LA had done almost nothing with my case, but they did find out one piece of evidence they shared with my dad and I. It appeared my sleeping partner had been entering my apartment by simply picking my door handle lock with a credit card. This was a tactic I regrettably did myself before when I was locked out and never really thought about how vulnerable it revealed the security of my apartment to be.

My dad had actually been doing more work on the case than the cops but he didn't tell me much about it until reluctantly came home for Thanksgiving. My nerves had been soothed by the gin and tonics the two of us had been swigging after our holiday gorging and I had opened up to discussing the painful incident.

"There were actually security cameras outside of your door in the hallway of your building," my dad said after a long discussion about whether I was comfortable with even talking about the whole thing.

"Now that you mention it, I do remember that," I said.

"Yeah, the cops didn't even look at it as far as I could tell," my dad groused. "But I did. According to your building's manager, they hadn't worked in a couple of years, but they just left them there broken. They got the security company to turn in the old tapes to the cops, but there was nothing showing the guy coming to your apartment in the night. But I had been wondering... you said you had gotten into your apartment before by picking the lock with a credit card, did you ever tell anyone about that?"

"As far as I can remember, no, and if I did it would have been a close friend. It was literally like five years ago though."

Judging by how furiously my dad started sucking down his drink, I could tell he was on to something.

"If it was five years ago, those security cameras still worked. They would have seen you do it."

My dad started chewing on his gin-washed ice, I finished the last of my drink.

"They also would have known the cameras didn't actually work the past couple of years," I chimed in.

We sat there silently for a few more moments before I asked another question.

"What was the name of the security company?"

———————————

Alta Rose Security's office was tucked into the middle of the endless sun-bleached field of warehouses and factories that was City of Industry, California. The hideous white stucco building the company took residence in looked possibly abandoned when my dad and I walked up to the heavily-barred front door.

My dad dialed up the listed extension for Alta Rose on a filthy little call box next to the door. Without a word from the other end, the box made a muffled noise and the black-barred door gave a hearty buzz.

We entered a dark, stuffy little hallway that smelled like a mix of chlorine and the ghosts of cigarettes that led us to a thick mahogany door for Alta Rose.

I followed my dad inside the office.

The inside of the office looked like an episode of hoarders. Dusty cardboard boxes were stacked all around the lobby like a game of office Jenga, the floor was littered with loose folders and random papers and decrepit-looking office equipment. I watched my dad almost fall on his ass after tripping over a three-hole puncher.

"Hello," my dad called out in a thoroughly-annoyed tone.

It took a while, but eventually a woman's voice responded behind a dead computer monitor.

"Yes, come in."

My dad and I followed the voice up to a front counter and an elderly woman wearing heavy red eye shadow, Rouge and bright red lipstick which made her look a bit like a clown stood up with her big hoop earrings jangling.

She peered at us from behind gold glasses and smacked her lips.

"Not sure if you have the right office. We went out of business two weeks ago."

"Oh no, no, no problem," my dad replied. "We are actually just looking to ask some questions."

My dad's words sounded distant in my ears. I was distracted by something I saw on the wall next to the woman – a framed portrait plaque. The plaque featured a younger man of about 30 with long black hair, a gaunt white face with sunken eyes and an unsmiling mouth. There was no denying it. It was my sleeping partner from the videos. I noticed an inscription upon gold below the picture – EMPLOYEE OF THE MONTH SCOTT LYNN.

"Uh, uh, uh ma'am," I could barely get the words out. "Where is he?"

I pointed to the plaque of Scott Lynn with a wobbling hand and the woman squinted up at the thing.

My heart dropped when she spoke.

"That's Scott. Worked here for years but left a few months ago and moved to Atlanta, but I don't know why."

3

Letter I

My cousin received the first letter at our apartment in Atlanta with no return address while I lived there. She shared the letter with my dad, but held off on telling me because she didn't want to make my life even worse and didn't think it would help with actually catching Scott. I wouldn't discover the letter until almost a year later when I was checking in with the police about the situation as apparently my dad had thought the same way that my cousin did and never shared it with me either.

The police eventually showed me the letter, scrawled in chicken-scratched pencil, the letter was written on the back of a printed-out boarding pass for a past flight from Los Angeles to Atlanta and dated just before Thanksgiving when I headed home for the holiday.

November 24th
Dear Katherine –
I never meant it to be like this. The last thing I ever wanted to do was scare you. I always thought you would find out someday, but I never thought it would be that way. I never wanted you to have to leave your life behind and start somewhere new.
That was the last thing I wanted to do.
But I was even more scared about how my explanation would

change your life and that's why I had to do what I did and why I never said anything. I wanted to all those years, but I could just never bring myself to do it. Laying my eyes on you had been such a divine miracle of justice that I didn't even know how to react and I didn't want to break the connection we were able to forge by telling you my secret, so I just laid there every night, feeling truly content for the first time in my life.

I don't expect you to ever fully understand, I just hope someday I will work up the courage to tell you.

Happy Thanksgiving,

Scott

4

December

My dad gulped. I could tell he was going to say something he really didn't want to say.

"I haven't been completely honest with you. There's something I need to show you."

The video my dad pulled up on his laptop couldn't have looked more innocent at first. I was watched a trio of preteen boys I vaguely recognized from the neighborhood throw down slam dunks into a water basketball hoop in a sun-drenched suburban backyard.

"Russell Miller from down the street's dad gave me this video a few months ago."

I was about to ask my dad why I would care about Russell Miller and his little buddies holding a pool slam dunk contest, but was interrupted by the bright scene getting interrupted by a close-up of Russell breathing hard in the dark of night.

He started to talk in between labored breaths.

"We're eggin' every house up and down this block. No one is safe I swear, not even that big ass guy down the block with the scary ass German Shepherd."

The video cut to a darkened shot of the front of my parents' house slightly obscured by some bushes. The sound of young boys panting heavily served as the soundtrack until Russell stepped into the shot with an egg in his hand and snickering filled the air.

Russell cocked back his arm to launch and I watched the first couple of eggs splatter just above my childhood bedroom window. He grabbed a couple more eggs out of the pocket of his hoodie and readied to launch them.

He stopped.

"What the fuck, bro?" he whispered and ducked back down behind the camera.

"What happened? What happened?" the cameraman asked.

"There's someone out there. I think I just hit him with an egg," Russell whispered, his eyes glued to my parents' house.

The camera panned through the brush and focused in on my parents' house shining in the pale street light. It took a second for the shot to focus, but my breath disappeared once it did.

Standing off to the side of my parents' house, crouching down next to small shrubs was the unmistakable darkened silhouette of a man.

Scott.

"What the hell is he doing?" the voice of the cameraman whispered.

Just as the cameraman finished talking, Scott's gaze turned towards the bushes where the boys were hiding.

"Holy shit. Holy shit!" the boys' voices cried out over the final frames of the video.

I looked to my dad with tears in my eyes. He looked like a dog that had just been scolded for going through the trash.

"Why didn't you tell me?"

"I didn't want to make you feel even worse."

"What the fuck, Dad?"

"And there's something else I found out I haven't told you about yet. I found out our home security company was owned by the same company Scott Lynn worked for, Alta Rose. It just had a different name. I didn't know, but it might mean he could…"

"Tweak your security system," I said with disgust in my voice. "How did you let this happen?"

"There was nothing I could do."

The morning air in my parents' living room suddenly grew cold upon my skin. I thought I could never feel worse than I did a few days ago when we found out about Scott's move to Atlanta in that cramped little office, but I did. I couldn't believe I had been living at my parents' house for so much of the time when Scott was lurking at least outside of the house, and maybe even inside.

"Do you think he got in the house?"

"I have no idea. There are no cameras or anything in here, just the alarm system, but I swear to you, I check every inch of this house in the morning, when I get home from work and before I go to sleep. Even the guest room. I swear to you Katherine."

———————————

It was fitting that Scott looked so much like a ghost, because for all intents and purposes, he was. The cops started taking my case a little more seriously when it was revealed Scott had followed me to Atlanta, but they couldn't find out a single thing about him.

The cops found no birth or census records for Scott. The

paperwork they got from the security company was light and contained what was believed to be mostly false information. His name may not have actually been Scott Lynn for all anyone ever knew. The only information anyone got was from the security company who was able to track down a technician who said he got drinks with him a few times after work and said he liked whiskey sours.

I was not the least bit surprised, but Scott also had zero social media presence at all. This confirmed my theory that everyone under the age of 35 who has zero social media presence is probably some kind of violent or sexual criminal.

Well... that's not entirely true. Scott had a social media presence, it just wasn't his own.

Immediately after hearing about Scott's move to Atlanta I started doing social media digging into my cousin Felicia. Despite my pleas of never putting me on her profiles, Felicia would still occasionally put pictures of me on Facebook or Instagram in various group shots.

I was reviewing Felicia's posted photos from the past few months to see how many I was in and if there was some way I could be tracked in them when I noticed something that would make my stomach drop just the same way it had when I watched the video of Scott lying next to me. There was a presence in nearly every recent picture Felicia had posted on social media that included me in an open public place in the past few months... the silhouette of Scott.

There we were, smiling in the park for a friend's birthday and a tall, slender, dark-haired figure lurked in the distant background. At a darkened bar, there he was off in the distance saddled up in a stool. The last picture I clicked upon was the worse. A small get together with friends in the grassy courtyard of the apartment building where I lived with Felicia, I could see a faint figure walking on the sidewalk across the street from where we were picnicking.

I couldn't even handle it anymore. I wanted to throw the laptop across the room, go up to my room, curl up and die. I felt helpless against everything. I didn't even feel safe in the room I grew up in with the door locked. Worse yet, I didn't truly trust my dad anymore. Why had he not told me about the video of Scott outside of their house when he first got it? I felt like he was truly just trying to protect me, but did it in the wrong way.

Maybe this was why mom lost her mind all of those years ago?

This is where I have to explain I haven't been completely honest while telling this story and why I can't completely call my dad out without feeling like a hypocrite. I may have been referring to the house as my parents' house, but it had pretty much just been my dad's house for the past 14 years.

We never figured out exactly what it was. After a lot of waffling, the doctor's eventually just said my mom had a stroke. I thought it was extremely early onset Alzheimer's or late onset schizophrenia, but what the hell did I know? I was just a teenager. Regardless, 14 years ago my mother completely changed. She went from being an outgoing social and financial stallion who was a partner at a law firm, to a nearly bed ridden shut-in that had a lot of trouble forming coherent sentences.

I was young, but I could tell my dad didn't really know what to do. There was nothing too physically wrong with my mom.

I guess her blood pressure and cholesterol ended up being a little high and she had to take medication for it, but other than that, all of her problems appeared to be with communication.

What ended up happening with her pains me to even try and explain. I try to hate my dad for it sometimes before I am able to convince myself I wouldn't really know what to do in the situation either. My mom ended up moving to the guest room down the hall from mine. For the past 14 years, my mom has spent 99.9 percent of her time in that room mostly lying in bed and watching TV. Every once in a while she would come downstairs to get food, but mostly my dad just brought it to her. As far as I knew, she had never left the house during the entire 14-year stretch.

Whenever I was home, I would go into her room and talk to her for at least a few minutes or so, but it was not easy. She would get very upset when even me and I my dad got too far into the room and all she seemed to be able to talk about was what was directly going on in the room, or what was on TV. Usually our conversations revolved around her complaining about the color of the walls of the room, a loud toilet or some Doctor Oz bullshit. It was fucking awful.

I could tell my social media revelations rattled my dad just as much as they did me because he immediately called the police and screamed at them right next to me for 10 minutes about how they should have an officer permanently parked outside of our house at night. He also called Felicia with me and demanded she follow my routine of living at her parents' house in the suburbs of Atlanta until Scott was apprehended. I asked my dad if he could also follow up with the family lawyer about a restraining order we had tried to file against Scott, but he reminded me that you cannot file a restraining order against someone who technically doesn't appear to exist on paper.

My next demand to my dad was we go spend the night in a hotel, but he wouldn't move on it either. His explanation was understandable. He didn't want to leave my mother in the house alone and there was no way in hell she was going to go stay at a hotel. He didn't want me going to stay in a hotel without him either.

My dad came up with a solution that worked for me. He spent the rest of the afternoon scouring the Internet for the scariest-looking private investigator he could find in the LA area. We settled on an Armenian guy named Buddy who looked like a cartoon henchman and had excellent reviews on Yelp. Before nightfall, Buddy was parked on the curb in front the house in a black Cadillac chain vaping and listening to hardcore rap.

Buddy's presence and the appreciation I had for my dad spending the entire day helping me had soothed me enough to where a few drinks over the dinner we ordered from my favorite pizza place from childhood sounded like a good idea. The herby-sweet gin and tonics my dad knew how to mix up so well were working like chamomile tea to my haunted soul.

The world's oldest sleeping medication, alcohol, had done the trick. Not long after dinner, I climbed the stairs up to my room with such exhaustion I could barely conquer the handful of steps.

Utterly gassed, I stumbled into my room, shut the door and locked in behind me and tucked myself into bed.

I awoke to the sound of feet shuffling outside of my bedroom door.

I had managed to fall asleep for the first time since I had heard about Scott's move to Atlanta, but my slumber didn't last long. An alarm clock that read 12:34 am meant I hadn't even been asleep for an hour

The amount of alcohol made me a little calmer than I should have been, but was still right back on edge for the most part. I jumped up out of my bed and scrambled for the pepper spray which now permanently rested on my nightstand. My eyes shot over to the little slice of light that cut through the crack in the bottom of the door, but there was nothing there.

A touch more at ease, I jumped back upon the bed and sat up with my back against the headboard. I tried to catch my breath and ease for a moment and focused my eyes on the moonlit window.

I immediately noticed something out of the ordinary with the window. There was something slimy and shimmery stuck to the top of the window with little flecks of something white in it. I got up from the bed and took a closer look. I could tell what it was right away. It was an exploded egg.

The sight of the egg took me back to a hazy memory of the night before – awaking for a brief moment after hearing a couple of thumps. It was one of those memories that you at first aren't really sure if it was a dream or real because it was so brief and clouded by the blanket of boozy sleep.

This memory sparked a realization... the video my dad showed me wasn't really from months ago. It was from last night. It made much more sense. The neighborhood kid had probably been caught last night and his parents probably gave my dad the incriminating video this morning.

There were footsteps again, but this time there were shadows of feet in the crack beneath my bedroom door.

I let out a shallow scream and ran back over to the pepper spray.

"Katherine," I recognized the voice that whispered through the door so quietly I could barely hear it.

It was my mom.

"Mom?" I whispered back.

My mom quickly jumped into her usual cadence. She could say words, brief sentences about something recent in her environment, but it was always patchy and vague.

"Skinny. Fucker. I can't smile," my mom started in.

I wanted to ask for something more. More clarity, but I knew it was hopeless, I just let her go on into my door.

"He's, he's, he's, he is," she stuttered. "He is staying. Ugly black hair."

All it took was that last line to make me know what my mom was talking about and realize another lie my dad had told me. He had said he checked every inch of the house when he did his thorough search of the house earlier every day, but probably never checked my mom's entire room. My mom would physically attack you with her rarely-clipped nails if you did too much prodding in her room. I bet he just opened the door and called it good.

I frantically thought of where my cell phone was to call the police. Quickly realized I had left it downstairs in my drunken absentmindedness.

My mother's voice interrupted my frantic scrambling.

"He's been in room. Days. I think, looking, for you."

Just as my mom finished, another pair of shadowy feet appeared in the bottom crack of the door and I screamed as loud as I could.

I heard the door to the master bedroom down the hallway shaking like it was holding back a caged rhino. The sound of my dad wailing against the door drowned out some more disjointed statements from my mom and what sounded like the faint whispering of a man. I wanted to scream at my dad to shut the fuck up so I could hear what the man who I assumed was Scott whispered into the door, but didn't get the chance.

The racket coming from the direction of my dad's door came to a head and I heard my dad's feet stomp down the hallway and fly down the stairs. I listened to my dad tearing about the first floor of the house over the sound of my heaving breathing and my mother making eerie statements.

"Can't watch you go," my mother said just outside of the door.

"Fuck," I heard the single word burst out of my dad's mouth from the first floor before I heard him run back up the stairs.

"Katherine," his voice boomed through the door followed by ragged breaths.

"What the fuck just happened?" I asked.

"He got out the back door."

"Scott?"

"I don't know. I didn't see him. He shoved a cabinet against my bedroom door. I had to break it down with a golf club."

I didn't respond.

"Can you open the door? It's okay, it's just me and your mom out here."

I turned the lock and opened the door to reveal my dad standing shirtless in the hallway with my mom behind him.

He looked upon me with sweat beading down his face.

"He slipped out into the woods out back. Buddy is following him. You can come out if you want."

I thought about it silently for a moment. I stared at my sweating dad and my raving derelict mother who was fidgeting about behind him.

"No, that's okay. I'm just going to stay in here for the rest of the night."

I started to shut the door, but noticed something in my dad's hand... a crumpled piece of paper.

"What's that?" I asked with my eyes on his hand.

"Oh, uh, just something I found. Just some trash."

"Can I see it?"

"Sure," my dad answered in a tone that made it clear he was reluctant to give me the paper.

I wrung out the lined notebook paper that had been crumpled into a ball in my dad's hand. A quick glance revealed it was a note, scribbled in tragically sloppy handwriting with an eye liner pencil Scott must have snagged from my mom's bathroom.

I know someday you'll have a beautiful...

It cut off there. Scott was probably in the midst of writing his note when my dad made it out of his bedroom and he had to dart away, leaving me with just those seven words that would haunt me for years.

5

Letter II

It turns out that first letter wasn't the only one that my dad had shared with the police, but not me. After reading the first, the officer asked me if I wanted to read the rest of them and proceeded to lead me to a stack of papers of a height which immediately raised the goosebumps on my entire body. The stack of wrinkled papers must have been at least six inches thick and I could see the familiar lead scribblings on the top one almost shining in the light of the station when I walked up to the desk and started reading the top one.

December 23rd

Katherine –

I'm sorry for my persistence, but I am especially drawn to you this time of year. It seems when the weather gets colder and the stores fill with sentimental pieces of dyed plastic is when I feel the loneliest and long for you the most. My bed just feels so cold on these nights now. I shiver beneath my covers trying to remember the warmth of your bed on all of those nights when I wasn't alone. Those years of relief in my life provide me with some lightness in my heart after all the years of horrible torture in the night that I always feel might come back as long as I am alone.

I try not to think of the nights at the home by the cold river the most. *They were the coldest, but most of the time the cold were the least of my troubles. I think I fear nighttime, bedtime the most, because that's when they would come, when I was alone in the dark. That crack of light that would leak into the room when the door opened pushed tears out of my eye sockets and my body would tense up, wishing it could fight against what would come next, but I was far too small, weak. It's no wonder I always have to sleep with the lights on if I am alone.*

But I had no choice back then. I was sentenced to bed and then had to just wait there for my punishment in the night. I still can feel that cold sting of the river every night when I shiver with loneliness and pain. That night I tried to escape by swimming across the frigid river like a prisoner. We had watched that movie on the TV where the prisoners tried to escape Alcatraz and we tried to give it a go. Some of us didn't make it and they may have been the lucky ones, because the ones who got rescued before the hypothermia fully took hold had to go back to the home.

That fucking home by the river where the music never stopped playing. That fucking place. I came back in the middle of the night one night not that long ago and left a cigarette burning on the porch in a puddle of gas in hopes that it would set the place ablaze, but no. I drove by the next morning and just the porch had been scorched, the hideous guts of that rusty trailer remained in its blanket of wet trees. Maybe the evil in there was indestructible.

It was so horrible I feel bad even telling you about it, but I feel like I have to. Maybe then, you will understand why I am the way that I am. What happened to me? I was not born this way. I was made this way and I can't help it. I am sorry.

Merry Christmas,
Scott

I furiously flipped to the next letter to discover it was not in fact a letter. It was a sloppy work of art.

Sketched in the same smudged pencil lead that penned the letters, the drawing was eerily childish, scrawled in a stick figure style. The focus of the piece was a bed and resting on the bed were two stick figure characters, one tagged with long hair and feminine eyelashes, another with shaggy hair and a huge, ear-to-ear smile. The two were tucked up tight in a blanket and lying below a framed picture of what looked to be a buck deer.

I could only look at the crude drawing for a few minutes, it made me feel as if I had suddenly been coaxed into taking too stiff of a shot at a bar – fluid built up at the back of my tongue and my jaw started to loosen. Obviously I had actually lived out these drawings, but seeing them portrayed so intimate and sloppy seemed to sicken me even more. The drawings looked like something you would doodle during a college lecture when you bored with your idle mind and sleeping with some stranger in their daydreaming twisted my stomach and esophagus.

I flipped the paper to reveal an almost exact sketch.

Flipped another. Same thing. Again. And Again. And again. There were probably about 20 straight pages of just that same sketch in shimmering lead staring back at me from the cold paper.

I pushed all of the letters and drawings off of the table and watched them through the lens of salty tears. My tears fluttered softly to the cold linoleum floor like dead leaves from a tree and scattered around looking like some the notes from some kind of class that would teach you how to be a childish psychopath.

I shivered out a few more sobs with my eyes glued to the scattered papers before I noticed something new. It was a letter I had not seen, written on the back of one of the drawings.

I crouched down onto the floor to read the note on the back of the drawing, but was interrupted by a door frantically opening from behind me. I turned around swiftly to see an officer barging through the door looking red-faced and pissed.

"Who let you in here," the officer barked and stopped himself just above me with his hands on his hips.

"Wait, what?" I screamed before I tore at the papers in front of me.

The officer grabbed my arms before I could snatch up any of the papers or read the note I was trying to read. He pulled me out of the room kicking and screaming with my eyes glued to that unread note until I was carried completely out of the room.

6

April, many years later

My mom got better. The key indicator to me was she was regularly unearthing memories from long before she disappeared into a fog of dementia and she seemed to be able to communicate in a way that didn't make it seem she was a dyslexic reading cue cards.

The night Scott appeared in my parents' house and then escaped into the night was almost three years ago and I had had effectively scrubbed away a lot of what happened. It was now like a movie you only saw once a long time ago, I remembered the plot and some images, but not the details.

A big part of why it felt like another life was I had moved on to a completely different life after the in-house incident with Scott. I heard about a unique opportunity which could jettison me and my mom far from LA and provide safety. A giant out of commission mental hospital in Washington State tucked into the foothills of the Cascade Mountains had reopened as an outpatient living facility for those living with mental disabilities and their family members. In an effort to promote support for mental illness the facility was offering very generous rates for those who would like to come live in the community.

It was a fantastic deal. I shared a little, two-bedroom bungalow with my mom. My dad paid the yearly bill and I worked part-time at the facility refurbishing the grounds and buildings that had yet to be remodeled. Only about a quarter of the facility was livable when we made our trek up North and they needed people like me to take care of their loved ones and do the remodeling of the rest of the facility in their spare time.

This living situation might sound creepy, especially for someone who had spent a chunk of their life unknowingly sleeping with a stranger, but it made sense to me. I was no longer really interested in participating in the real world of offices and rented apartments. Scott had tracked me down in two major metropolitans and beaten the expensive home security system in my parents' McMansion anyways. This opportunity would allow me to shave some of my personal guilt about my mother away by helping her, give me some income and let me live in a secluded place with tight security.

Besides, the facility could not have been more beautiful. Classic and sprawling, the massive facility cut into a forest of thick evergreens and was remodeled by interior design students from a local college as part of an internship program. Overflowing with classic architecture, mood lighting, exposed brick and flowing ivy, the place looked like something out of a European fairy tale romance.

My days had turned into a nice little routine. I woke up around 10:30, made coffee for my mom and I and we sat on our porch facing a lush courtyard with a colossal fountain that looked like it belonged on a street corner in Rome. We would usually sit for an hour or so discussing the past – my mom's life before she met my dad, my childhood – until the last drops in our coffee mugs were long cold. I then went to work on the facilities for the afternoon and when done, spent the night cooking a nice dinner in the bungalow with my mom before we watched TV or movies until we fell asleep.

I wasn't completely alone with my mother. I had made a friend. Carson was a security guide at the facility who seemed to be the only other person on the entire campus who was under the age of 40. He was a mountain of a man who had at least 10 inches and 100 pounds on me, but held it all softly. He was like a giant teddy bear complete with ears that stuck out to the side and a permanent smile.

My friendship with Carson started when he brushed past me one day on campus and I noticed the distinct smell of marijuana upon him. It took a while, but I eventually slid into a comfortable conversation with him while we were in line in the cafeteria. Before you knew it, we were ducking off into the jogging trails carved into the woods to vape just about every day.

It was the first time I had formed a true relationship of any kind with someone in the past three years and even though I was still apprehensive, it could not have felt better. The fact Carson was objectively a gentle soul made it really easy as well. One time we had planned to meet out in the jogging trails to vape in the afternoon and I got there a little earlier than anticipated to find Carson knelt down, cradling a mouse which had been maimed by a bird. I stayed off in the distance and listened to the man who looked like an NFL offensive lineman speak soft comforting words to the tiny animal before he tucked it into his pocket once he heard me walking in his direction.

It was these kinds of things that always made me feel safe

with Carson. The fact we were smoking in what in my humble opinion was the creepiest area of the entire campus was an absolute testament to how much I trusted him. Some people may have been terrified more of the long abandoned mental hospital rooms which still had the chairs where people were strapped down and lobotomized, but it was the jogging trails that got me.

The jogging trails were sawdust-floored paths that weaved through the woods which surrounded the facility like the veins in your arms. Shaded by the towering evergreens above, the trails were dark even on the sunniest of days and sprawled for acres in a shadowy maze that seemed to have no right or reason what so ever. The trails were such a twisted labyrinth it was actually suggested by facility staff numerous times they be closed off and at the very least not be allowed to be used if you were by yourself. They were so long Carson said they could be reached by a short walk through the woods by his house a few miles away.

It was on those shadowy paths I would get my first true therapy. Carson and I walked the trails together each afternoon smoking and soothing our brains. I would talk about my life while excluding the details about Scott and he would tell me about his horrific, but enthralling life growing up in foster homes in the rural forests of Washington state. It seemed like whenever I was tempted to divulge my own dark secrets to him, he would tell me a new story that lowered the bar for how bad people can be to children and I had to tuck my own problems back into an entitled folder.

I had formed a deep, deep bond with Carson, but I wasn't sure what the exact emotion tied to it was. Love? I don't know.

I had an utter fondness for him and I could tell he did for me, but I also wasn't sure what emotion he was attaching to me either. It had been more than a year that we had been having our vapes and talks but he had never made even the slightest of moves. It was charming, but also unattractive at the same time. If he truly had feelings for me, he was not going about it the right way.

One rainy afternoon it appeared Carson was going to make a move. I ran through the torrential rain to the safe cover of the tall trees which roofed the jogging trails where Carson and I had planned our usual smoke sessions. He told me to meet him there a little later than usual because he had to head to town to pick up some supplies for the office, but his true intention for our delayed meeting was immediately clear when I stepped into the near darkness of the forest and noticed candlelight.

Perched just a few handfuls of yards into the trails were two polyester folding camping chairs and a little wooden table lined with a few candles which added the scent of gardenias to the dense aroma of herby evergreens and wet foliage. Waiting for me in one of the chairs and wearing the biggest smile I have ever seen in my life was Carson.

The first thing Carson did was present me a copper mug filled to the brim with an ice cold Moscow mule. Alcohol was the absolute number one forbidden piece of the contraband on the facility, so this was an extra special treat and a show of excellent memory by Carson. I had once mentioned about a year ago Moscow mules were one of the top things I missed from my LA life and that copper mugs were an absolute must.

The drink hit me hard. I hadn't had a sip of alcohol in years. It was like being 16 again – lush drunk and giddy.

"Let's go somewhere," the words clumsily tumbled out of my drunken mouth after I downed the last drops of my first drink.

I knew the exact problem Carson was doing the math on in his head. Employees of the facility and residents were not supposed to interact outside of the grounds – especially residents who had been plied with banned substances. Also, the only town within reasonable driving distance had a population of only 2,000 who all seemed to work at the facility and knew each other. This left Carson with one option so I wasn't the least bit surprised when he responded to me with this question.

"Want to just go to my house?"

Our operation seemed like something out of a spy movie. I piled into the very back of Carson's Explorer, covered myself with a sleeping bag and we drove out of the facility after a quick check in with the front gate guard.

I burst out into childish laughter as soon as we were far enough away from the entrance to where I could emerge from the cover of the sleeping bag and climb up into the passenger's seat next to Carson. I had not ridden in a car since I arrived at the facility so the experience kind of felt like riding on a roller coaster as Carson commanded the vehicle on the winding road that meandered upon the hill above the facility.

Carson's house was an algae-crusted eye sore made of dark wood, hidden down a black road. The house was centered in a small clearing of mossy ash trees whose bases were spotlighted by the headlights of Carson's SUV when we pulled into his muddy driveway.

I should have been scared, but the double shot of vodka in the Moscow mule was giving me confidence and Carson's romantic gestures were drowning my fears. I followed Carson out of the car and up steep stairs to the front door of his rustic home.

The second Moscow mule I sipped on as I sat on a worn couch put me at ease with the dated eeriness of Carson's living room. The soundtrack of soft rock music helped as well, along with the hulking body of Carson stretched out next to me onto the couch.

Our house party started out exceptionally well. It could not have felt more refreshing to be anywhere else other than the facility. Even though I loved my life there, the stagnation of the place wore on me.

The only thing bugging me was I noticed we had been listening to the same song now for nearly an hour when Carson got up to make our third round of drinks.

I wasn't sure what song it was, but it sounded like what I recognized vaguely as Pearl Jam. I had no idea what the lyrics were, but I kind of recognized the chorus and I could tell by the urgency of the music and the lead singer's voice the song was coming to an end.

After the final chorus, the song had a painfully intense moment when the lead singer broke his usual cadence and sang some tragic final words I didn't remember until I heard them trickling out of the computer in the corner of the room.

I know someday you'll have a beautiful life,
I know you'll be a star in somebody else's sky,

But why, why, why can't it be, can't it be mine?

I instantly recognized the first line from Scott's note he wasn't able to finish back at my parents' house.

"Why is this song on repeat?" The question shot off my tongue rapid fire in the direction of the kitchen where Carson was making our drinks.

"Uh, yeah, sorry. That's my roommate's computer, I forgot it was on. He's obsessed with that song for some reason. You know, you can probably turn that off, I'm pretty sure he's upstairs asleep."

My body's pulse of tension glued me to the couch as Carson finished.

"I'll go check."

I heard Carson's massive form trudge up the stairs in a sprint and then I heard a crash and a hideous scream.

I flew off of the couch and towards the front door. I made it there in a few leaping steps and threw a look over my shoulder as I opened the rickety wooden thing. I my frenzied glimpse, I saw a flash of Scott running out of the kitchen.

I burst out the front door, rumbled down the steps of the front porch and felt a downpour of rain fall upon me once I started sprinting away from the house. I heard furious feet pounding after me when I ran through the driveway in the direction of the dark woods.

One memory stuck out in my head as I pumped my arms and legs as fast as I could in the night – Carson had mentioned the jogging trails were a short distance from the woods around his house. I wasn't exactly sure what direction from the house the trails would be, but I figured continuing my strides in a straight line towards the trees would be my only really shot no matter where they were.

I put my head down and pressed on with the sound of Scott's feet still behind me.

After ripping through a few shrubs and branches about 20 yards into the forest, I discovered I had played my cards right. I found myself sprinting down the soggy wood ships of the jogging paths with the sound of heavy rain beating down upon the dark canopy of the tops of the trees above me. I took no time to check if Scott was still trailing me, just kept sprinting into the blue near darkness, hoping the path I was on would lead me towards the facility.

I could only maintain my speed for a few more minutes. I soon found myself stomping through the soggy wood shavings at a much slower pace with my mouth heaving out labored breaths. Unable to move much further without vomiting and with no sounds of footsteps trailing me, I slowed to a brisk walking pace and shot a look over my shoulder.

There was nothing there. Just the tumbling of heavy raindrops working their way down from the leaves of the trees above.

Without any threats in sight, I came to a complete stop to catch my breath for a moment and assess the situation. I may not have been able to see Scott, but he could have been anywhere, and regardless, I was far from out of the woods (literally), even if he had given up on me and returned to his home. I knew first hand just how big of a maze the jogging trails were and I was at the very far end of them, a few miles from the safety of the facility at best. On top of that, there was a more than good chance Scott was still pursuing me in the dark twisting arteries of the trails. If he was, it was only a matter of time until the unpredictable paths the trails led us on crossed in the dark.

I pressed on as swiftly as my body would let me, maintaining a steady jog. My chest heaved and heart raced. My brain was tested as well. The two drinks had faded from my mind and left me in a hazy fog of mental fatigue. Combine that with only a little tickle of moonlight which pushed its way through the canopy of trees to give me just a soft hue of light on my journey and the whole thing felt like I was running through some endless nightmare in my own head.

A snap of brush from the outside of the path just in front of me sent my reflexes into a panic.

I stopped just before I crashed into a deer. I screamed in the poor things face and it galloped away into the night, leaving me stiff and wide eyed in the jogging path.

I used the opportunity to catch my breath for a moment, but it was a mistake. I heard the splashing of footsteps come up from behind me on the path. My scream must have given me away.

Without a look, I took off again going forward, but soon had to dart to the right when the path made a Y.

It was another poor choice. The path I had chosen was steeply uphill and I quickly lost steam.

Behind me, I could hear the splashing footsteps gaining on me, but there wasn't anything I could do, the grade ahead of me was a challenge and it would be a few more yards before I crested the slope. The math taking place in my head told me the steps behind me would soon be upon me…

But then they stopped.

I started to whip my head around to check on what may or may not have been behind me, but stopped. There was a figure ahead of me, just past the top of the crest of the path. It was hard to make it out, but it was tall, dressed in white and stepping up to me at a steady pace.

It was Scott.

I started to backpedal, but it was too late, Scott had the higher ground and was just a few yards away from me. His dark eyes grew wide when he laid them upon me and started picking up his pace.

"No. No. No. No," I cried out into the wet night, but I knew it was helpless.

I tripped backwards down the slippery slope of the path and fell hard upon my backside.

Scott strolled up to me and stepped down to stand over me, his lip quivered and his body shivered, cold.

He had something to say. His mouth started to open.

Before I could close my eyes or scream…

He was engulfed and taken out of sight.

I scrambled up to my feet and saw Carson wrestling with Scott in the brush next to the trail. I could hear both men yelling out incoherent curses until the much larger Carson fully gained control and pinned Scott on his back.

Carson started to pummel my frail stalker, but a flash of silver in the night caught my eye…

Scott wrestled a gun out of pocket.

"He's got a…

I didn't have to finish my warning, Carson twisted the barrel of the gun away from his face and towards Scott before what sounded to me like a bomb going off shook the woods. I turned away from the image of blood erupting from Scott's face.

"He tried to shoot me. You saw it. You saw it," Carson turned and yelled at me, his face covered in scratches.

At first, I couldn't get anything out. My jaw just quivered. Carson stepped away from Scott's lifeless body, came up to me and wrapped me in a hug.

It took a few moments, but I would eventually get some words out.

I cried into Carson's chest.

"Thank you."

The past few months were the most restful of my life since before I knew about Scott. Knowing he was officially dead and gone allowed for me to start returning to normal. I had started a full-time desk job at the facility, began quietly dating Carson and planned on bringing up getting an apartment in town together so we could date officially since I would no longer be a resident of the facility.

In a major step forward, I agreed to go on a road trip with Carson across the mountains and over to central Washington where he said the spring was warm and beautiful. I was sitting in his car waiting for him to finish his shift and enjoying the lush scenery out the passenger side window when I saw something that pulled at my heartstrings. A female deer stepped out of the cover of the forest by the jogging trails and out into a golden field behind the facility.

It looked exactly like the deer I ran into on the trails the night Scott was chased me. The deer wasn't alone – two spring fawns eventually followed it out of the woods. I grabbed my phone. A quick snap of my phone and the moment was saved forever.

I decided to share the moment with Carson. Immediately sent the picture to his phone. I jumped a little bit when a digital chime shot out from the cup holder next to my seat.

I snatched up his phone and saw a little notification that explained his phone was out of memory. He would have to delete some files to receive my picture.

Carson had some weird ass Windows Phone or something, so I wasn't exactly sure to work it, but after a little bit of playing around with it, I ended up on an album where I was presented with a screen of endless tile previews of photos and videos.

Figuring I would help him out and let him receive my amazing photo at the same time, I started scrolling through to find random photos and videos I was sure he could easily part ways with. I started with the oldest and scrolled my all the way back to a few years ago, around when I had just moved up to the facility.

The first handful of photos and videos I deleted were easy to spot – accidental photos of black taken within a pocket or quick videos taken but then aborted before they went anywhere. However, one of those quickly-aborted videos started to raise the little hairs on the back of my neck.

One of the quick little videos took place in the night, a few years ago, in a locale I knew very well. It was just a few seconds, but the little strip of grass behind my bedroom in the bungalow where I stayed was unmistakable.

The next video I pulled up would be much more terrifying. It was almost completely dark, but you could just barely make out what was going on… shot through the tiny little gaps in the blinds of my bedroom window, you could see my body tucked up in a sea of blankets, sleeping away in the night.

My reflexes threw the phone down to the floor and my muscles seized, I couldn't move. Much like the deer I had just been gazing upon would, I froze in the headlights of the oncoming threat. But my threat was not a racing automobile, it was a lumbering man whose footsteps I could hear sloshing through the gravel outside the car.

I nearly threw up when the driver's side door opened and Carson dropped behind the wheel. I could run. I could fucking run. But what the hell would that do? Carson had a gun. He shot Scott right in front of me with it. I knew he still carried it everywhere he went. Would he shoot me if I ran? Did I care? All of this flashed through my head in the few seconds before Carson spoke up next to me and I realized I should have been worrying about a part of Carson's security guard tool belt other than the gun.

His handcuffs.

The feeling of cold metal wrapping around my left wrist snapped me out of my frantic questioning. My eyes looked to Carson's, but his were stuck on the floor where his phone was still broadcasting a video of me sleeping.

Carson's cool blue eyes drifted back towards me, holding the same love they always had.

"This will all make sense eventually."

7

I don't know when

One of the great things about the human body and mind is how quickly you get used to things, no matter how awful they are. I had no idea exactly how long I had been locked in the room, but I was sure it was a long time and just few days into my imprisonment, I had already started to develop a few things a day that made me happy. The smell of coffee coming from somewhere else in the house just after sunrise, the sound of a cat scurrying across hardwood floors outside my door and the little crack of sunlight that cut through the boards which sealed the windows in my room on what I assumed were sunny days. I liked these things much more than the soggy Lean Cuisine's that slid underneath the wooden door of my room three times a day.

Carson put me in the room, but I could hear other people milling about the house all the time. Based on what I could hear, it seemed to me at least five people lived in the house, though it seemed they rarely came by my door other than to drop off the Lean Cuisine offerings. No one seemed to speak anywhere close to my door. I could only faint sometimes hear voices from a great distance in the house and sometimes outside.

I had no idea where the house was. Carson drove for hours with me handcuffed to the steering wheel of his car. He never said anything despite me screaming at him until I ran out of breath and despite me punching him with my free arm as hard as I could as many times as I could. He just kept staring out at the desolate road that wound through thick forest until the world turned the lights out on us and the headlights came on.

We eventually pulled into a farmhouse type home settled next to a lonely highway and he drug me into the house. He pulled me up into the room where I was trapped now like some kind of unglamorous Rapunzel without even a mirror to look at to see how horrible I looked. I would frequently try to somehow look at my reflection in the porcelain of the toilet in the bathroom connected to my room, but couldn't get anything other than a heavy feeling of pain for the tragedy my life had become.

I had not verbally conversed with another human being for however long I had been in the room. The only form of communication I once got was after I had spent a few minutes trying to pry the boards off of the windows. I was interrupted by a piece of paper sliding underneath the door. It informed me I was being monitored on camera so things like trying to escape were not safe activities. A book of crosswords then slid underneath the door with the phrase "try this instead" written on it.

The crosswords lasted for a few days. Tying my hair into various knots lasted a few days. Talking to myself and writing out and acting out plays in my head lasted a few days. Trying to remember all the words to my favorite songs lasted for a few days. Everything my addled brain created to try and stave off boredom always lasted for a few days, but then needed to be replaced by something else, until I encountered the first real action in my life in quite some time.

The sounds of the footsteps of children their whispering voices appeared outside of my door. They came sporadically, seemingly every couple of weeks or so and their words were never loud enough to where I could make anything out, but I would still rush over to the door and place my ear upon the wood, hoping to gather some information.

Eventually, I got interaction with the children. It seemed like the middle of the night (exact times of day were hard to tell) when I was woken by the shuffling and murmuring and then rousted from my bed by the sound of a soft knock upon the door.

I stumbled to the door in the dark and answered back with a hard knock that produced screeches and screams from the other side of the door. I followed it up with a soft "help me."

The sound of my hoarse voice was answered with the pitter pattering of numerous little feet sprinting away, leaving me dejected and alone in the darkness.

Those little feet and voices would come back just a few days later in the night. This time I could understand what they were saying.

"We heard a voice last time, I think it is a lady," the high-pitched voice of a little boy shook me from my half sleep.

A soft knock upon the door greeted me. I worked my way to my feet and tiptoed to the door. I could hear their little voices whispering through the thick wood of the door when I stepped up and placed my ear to it.

"Hello?" A little boy's voice spoke up on the other side.

"Hi," I replied quietly, fully knowing my captors were recording me.

"Aunt Kathy?" The boy's voice went on.

"What? No."

"Why are you locked in there?"

"I don't know."

The children murmured amongst each other for a few moments.

"I told you it was her," the little boy's voice announced to the other children.

Before he could go on, they all snapped into an instant hush.

Heavier footsteps started to pick up in volume from off in the distance. The sounds of the children changed to those of panic. My spirit sunk when I heard the little footsteps scramble away from the door, but felt a sliver of hope sneak into my soul when I saw a few pieces of paper slide underneath my door. I grabbed them as quickly as I could, tucked them into my shorts and ran back to the safety of the covers of my little bed.

I heard the heavy footsteps pound just outside my door. I regained my breath underneath the covers and prayed that they would walk away. I clung tight to the papers I kept stuck between my legs, hoping I wouldn't hear the bottom of the door open into the room and squeak against the hardwood floor. I remained like still for a couple of minutes before I heard the heavy footsteps clomp away and started to breathe normally again.

I pulled the papers out from my shorts but kept my head beneath the covers. I didn't want the camera to pick up what

I was trying to look at. The papers appeared to be a home-published book, created by young children.

The title jumped off the cover at me in black marker and all caps:

THE MONSTER IN THE ATTIC

About 10-pages thick the little novella had the crude cartoon of some kind of boogeyman-looking creature reaching up for the title text. Even in my imprisoned state, the thought of someone thinking me as something as ugly as I was looking at stung.

The book read a lot like an urban legend. It told the story of two brothers who lived in the woods who always heard strange noises coming from the attic of their house. The boys hear about a legend that talks about a monster who lives in the attic of their house from an older brother and they share the story with the other kids in their small town. The kids eventually band together and choose to face the monster, they walk up to the door of the attic where it lives, but then the story abruptly ended with a page that was nothing but just wild scribbles.

But a closer glance revealed they were not simply scribbles. Hidden in the vortex of the squiggly circles of crayon were sloppy letters, just below the service of the waxy lines.

They read:

I FOUND YOUR CROSSWORD PUZZLES IN THE TRASH. TELL ME YOUR STORY IN THE NEXT ONE THEY GIVE YOU?

My next book of crosswords could not come soon enough. I spent the next few days chewing my nails till they hurt and pulling at my hair.

I flew through the crossword book as soon as it slid underneath my door just like it had each week prior, but eventually stopped myself. They might think something was up if I slid my finished crossword book back so quickly. It pained me, but even though it only took about an hour to scrawl my story into the soft paper of the book, I held onto the thing for a few days, about as long as it usually took me to finish the books.

My heart fluttered the day when I saw my completed crossword slide out of my sight and heard footsteps carry it away. Those flutters weren't all of hope and joy thought, there was also the dark tickling of fear and apprehension. What if my captors opened up that crossword and saw my tale and my message of help? What if this was some kind of sick, twisted game or trap being perpetrated by my young pen pal?

What if I was never getting out of this place?

———————

The wait for a response was excruciating. My grasp on time had grown thin, but I felt as if it was at least a few weeks before I heard those little footsteps dash up to my door again. This time it was just one pair and this time it was in the early afternoon. A time I longingly identified as the time between the school bell and the arrival of parents home from work.

I ran up to the door with my heart racing.

"Hello," I frantically whispered into the door.

The person on the other end took so long to reply I feared for a second my worst nightmares were true and this young explorer was not there to help me.

But he spoke.

"You're Katherine?"

"Yes, yes, did you read my story?"

"Yeah, but I didn't understand some of the words. I'm nine."

"Can you help me?"

"I can, but I don't have very much time. They will be home soon."

"Who's they?"

"A lot of people live here, but the grown ups are the ones who have you up here."

"Carson?"

"One of them is named Carson."

"Can you let me out? Please?"

"I can't right now. They would know it is me. I am the only one here."

"Why am I in here? Do you know why?"

"Because you are Kathy…"

The little voice halted.

"I have to go."

"No, no, no, no."

The little feet dashed away. I heard the sounds of a truck engine rumbling outside of my window.

————————

Carson must have known I was talking to the little boy. He came to my door that night. His familiar voice trickled my ears through the wood of the door and made me sick to my stomach. I hadn't heard that awful drawl in so long and I didn't miss it in the least bit while it was gone.

"Katherine," he tried to make his voice sound soothing when he called my name, I saw right through it.

"KATHERINE," he gave the soft approach a rest.

"WHAT?" I screamed back.

"There are things you don't yet understand."

"Oh please stop with that. What does that even mean?" I seethed and sat up on my bed. "This isn't some game. This isn't some TV show. This is my fucking life and you are stealing it."

"You think I want to do this? You think I want you locked up in a room instead of just living with me? This isn't my choice."

Now I really started to get worried. Being locked up in a dark, strange room for months already had me pretty fucking scared, but this was a new layer. Carson was beyond sick in the head if he thought there was some other force in play that required him to kidnap me and lock me up in a woodsy dungeon.

"Oh shut up. I can't believe I trusted you. Fuck off," I screamed. "Just tell me why you are doing this?"

There was a long, heavy silence.

"I can't, but maybe these can?"

A thick stack of papers slid under the door. I heard Carson's heavy footsteps trudge away into the distance.

8

Letter III

The thick stack Carson pushed into the room was another letter from Scott. This one looked more like a manifesto than the previous sonnets or creepiness. There also didn't appear to be any works of art in this letter, just the scratching of pencil all the way up and down coffee-stained notebook paper, crumpled as if they had been pulled from the trash after the author had thrown them away.

December, Always
Katherine –
This will likely be the last letter I write you. I think it is time for me to move on. Or, more appropriately, for me to let you move on. I am sorry again for bringing so much chaos to your life. It was never my intention, but we have been over this before, yada, yada, yada, etc...

I need to tell you my story. Which is also your story. So I guess you could call it... our story.

I remember waking up scared in the middle of the night, as far back as from when I think I was just two or three years old. I know most people can't remember back that far, but I can and I think it was because it was the last time I had true happiness and comfort in my life.

But sometimes in the middle of the night, things would not be so happy and comfortable. I remember my little bedroom was tucked in the basement of the huge house, down in the cold, down by where I could hear the "beer refrigerator" humming all night. Down by where the wind would whip against my windows and wake me up cold and scared.

Scared from the night, I would run from my bed, upstairs and to your room. I remember opening your pink door as slowly as possible, hoping not to wake you up. I remember scurrying across the carpet of your room in my little socks with equal delicacy and slipping into your bed and tucking myself below your treasured collection of stuffed animals.

I was always so glad you were such a deep sleeper because I never wanted to actually wake you up. I just wanted to lay with someone else in safety and warmth, far from the horror of my basement room until the sun almost came up and the light would rescue me from the shadows of the night.

Most nights you wouldn't even notice that I would come sleep in your bed, but when you did, you didn't mind. Sometimes I would even awake to a tiny little knock on my door in the middle of the night to see you standing there in your pajamas, clinging to your favorite stuffed gray rabbit and we would go back to your room to fight off our childhood fears together.

But this would not last forever. It's funny that I remember those nights so well, yet, my annexation from the family is just a haze of pain, confusion and heartbreak. It came suddenly, I remember one day riding in the back of dad's car by myself and not recognizing where we were going. I asked and he told me home, but then we went to the airport. The sound of airplanes still makes me feel empty, hollow. He put me on a plane and told me someone would meet me when I landed to explain where I was going. Then he didn't even give me a hug, just handed me off to someone at the counter at the gate and I watched him walk away into the faceless crowd of travelers. I couldn't have been more than a little bit older than three years old and I was by myself in an airport watching my dad turn disappear into a sea of strangers.

I would get on a plane for the very first time and fly for what felt like forever, your sense of time is so much slower when you are young. When I landed, I was greeted by a couple I had never seen before who greeted me with a big, big hug that almost made things feel a little bit better. They waited a little while, but they eventually told me they were my new parents as we sat around the fireplace that heated their entire ugly trailer.

I was never told why mom and dad gave me up. I spent my formative years crafting reasons, but never seemed to find one that made sense. They always seemed to love me when we were together, but then one day suddenly everything changed. I had so many theories, so many would make sense for so long, but then would fall apart the more and more I thought about them.

A lot of times I wouldn't think about it though. As bad as that strange day where dad put me on a plane was, it was better than even the best days with my new family.

A hardened couple who lived in the rural mountains of Washington state, my new parents were strangely much older than mom and dad (far too old to have a child of my age), drank to no end and had a very misguided, shaky grasp on fundamentalist Christianity. They were also foster parents who perpetually filled that trailer with a traveling circus of unwanted children who not surprisingly all seemed to have horrible issues themselves.

Homeschooled, the only time I ever really got out of that moldy trailer was to go to a church which held three-hour services which seemed to be nothing but lectures about guilt I felt I didn't earn. My only relief finally game around age 10 when I met a horribly fat boy named Carson at church who had really old parents just like me.

Me and Carson bonded over crappy cartoon Sunday school books and games of baseball played with nearly-rotten apples and thick sticks we would find in his backyard.

After a few years of that, good news finally came in the form of a funeral for Carson's elderly mother. The passing of Carson's mother was supposed to leave him in just the care of his even more-elderly father, but deeming himself unfit to care for a growing boy who was eating him out of house and home, his father decided Carson should come live at the foster trailer with me and my revolving door of arsonists, future child molesters and autistic kids who would stab me with forks at the dinner table.

Getting to make Carson my brother was the one hint of joy I had in my upbringing. We would be able to talk to each other until the sting of the belt whipped upon our backsides almost nightly would go away. We would talk about the few girls at church we thought were cute and how we would eventually talk to them and we would talk about you.

I didn't even know what your name was. I didn't even know where mom and dad lived. I didn't even know sometimes if those first few years of my life happened or not, but something deep in my soul told me they did and I told Carson all about it.

I told him about our big house. I told him about those nights where when I was scared of nothing, where I would slip off to your room and have someone to comfort me. You became almost a myth to us. A normal life that we both dreamed of as we shivered in our cold sleeping bags on the rotting floor dreaming of some other kind of life. Katherine, you were a fairy tale. We actually made a book. It was called *Queen Katherine of Upstairs*. It tells your story, what happened to you and what we would do if we ever found you. Carson still has it.

I tried to ask my new parents a few times about my previous family, but they never would give me any answers. They would just say they forgot and that they didn't want me to find them. It was about the only thing I believed from them. Clearly my real family did want to rid me from them or they wouldn't have put me there.

But my new parents couldn't rid me of one key piece of information saved from my childhood – palm trees. I remembered the tall, waving palm trees that lined the streets which led to the airport that day I left and I eventually would recognize them in a movie which took place in Los Angeles.

So the day I turned 18 and was released from my parents, I set off for LA with nothing more than a few hundred dollars I had cobbled together over the years and a backpack with some clothes. I had no idea where my family could be in LA, but Carson had given me an idea, a brilliant idea. If I could get a job at a security company where I sat watching security cameras all day, I would have the best shot at seeing the most people over time and would have the best shot I could at eventually seeing dad, mom or you, even though I wasn't sure what you would exactly look like.

I was lucky enough to eventually get hired by a security company, but after years upon years of never seeing anyone that *looked anything like any of you, I gave up. I actually thought I had a better chance of running into one of you randomly so I wandered every mile of the city endlessly whenever I wasn't working, hoping to catch a glimpse.*

When it finally happened, it made me believe there is a god. Nothing but divine intervention could have led me to looking at the black and white footage of the boring old Hollywood adjacent apartment hallway security feed and seeing dad carrying boxes in and out of an apartment door and then seeing you, seeing a 25-year-old you, working with him.

Maybe even more unbelievable was what happened next, I got cold feet. I had waited all my life for this moment, dedicated my life to it and it had miraculously come and now I was scared. What the hell was I going to do? Walk up to you and say hi?

I couldn't? So I just watched you come and go from your apartment and it was enough for me for a while.

Until I saw you have to break into your apartment one day. So many things came together at once in my brain.

I knew I could break into your apartment.

I knew you were probably still a deep sleeper.

And I knew there was nothing I wanted more in life than to sleep next to you again.

So I did it.

And I never slept, just laid there, warm and content. Nothing more I needed in life. To just lie next to my family, my sister.

That is all,

Scott

9

Back in My Dungeon

The usually chilly room had grown strangely hot. I first connected the rise in temperature to my embarrassment and discomfort from reading Scott's letter, but the rising smell of ash and the sounds of crackling fire coming from outside my door changed my mind.

There was a fire heating up somewhere else in the house.

"Carson," I screamed into the door.

I got no answer. Just the rising sound and scent of burning ambers.

"Carson," I screamed again.

I heard the sound of heavy sobs start to rise over the chorus of the fire.

"CARSON!"

The sobs were interrupted by someone stammering with a full throat.

"I'm sorry. He always told me about how great you were and then I met you and you were even better. But I can't have you. And if I can't have you. No one can."

"No, no, no," I screamed and ran over to the door.

I pounded hard on the door. Carson's whimpers started to die down on the other side.

"Please," I screamed on.

"They're coming, I'm sorry," Carson said before I heard his feet dash away.

"No," I let out one last scream.

I scratched, pounded, pulled as hard as I could at the door, but it wouldn't budge. I ran back to the boarded windows, but I knew it was hopeless. I had pried at those things so many times and never gotten any of them to crack in the least. I was trapped in the fucking dungeon with the fire rapidly approaching my sealed door.

I searched the room for anything I could maybe use to attack the door or window boards, but couldn't find a single worthy tool. My entire body started to convulse as sudden hopelessness started to overcome me.

And then a pounding on the door wrestled away my surrender. The pounding was hard, but delicate at the same time and its softness instantly made me believe it belonged to somehow who might help and not harm.

I ran to the door and was greeted by a childish voice.

"Are you in there?" the young boy's voice called through the door.

"Yes, yes, yes, I am."

"Uh, the house is on fire, it's burning down, you need to get out, but I don't have the key to the lock."

"Shit."

"The fire is almost here. You could wait for it to burn the door down."

"That won't work, you need to break down the door. Get an axe or something."

"Okay, be right back."

The young boy's footsteps were drowned out by the sounds

of the now seemingly roaring fire. The crackles and snaps sounded like some kind of hideous bowl of Rice Krispies simmering just outside of the door.

"Hurry," I frantically muttered into the door. "Come on."

My pleading was interrupted by a heavy slamming upon the door which sent me to the floor in shock. I looked up to see the thick wood of the door splintered by the blood red of the head of an axe, the blunt, heavy object wiggled in the gashed wood before it disappeared and came back down again.

I wanted to rejoice. The young boy's Jack Torrance impression had me on the verge of seeing my first air outside of that fucking room in months and gave me a shot to escape the painful death of being burned alive. Thank God for the young boy whose name I still did not know. I don't know why, but my brain drifted to the rosy thoughts of a hot bath and a bottle of red wine.

But there was no time for daydreaming. Another chop of the axe ripped out nearly half of the door. I saw my savior's face for the first time.

Milky pale with a sloppy bowl cut of dark black hair that made him look a little bit like a pre-teen Beatle, the boy shared a striking resemblance with Scott. Even his dark eyes seemed to be directly pulled from my nightmarish image of my former sleeping companion and brother. He flashed a frothing mouth of half missing teeth as he looked me over for the first time.

"We gotta go," he screamed through the door. "Come on."

The young boy ripped some more wood out of the door. I

charged at the opening just as the axe came down again and nearly sent me to my feet.

"Sorry, you need more room," I heard his voice through the hole in the door. "Stand back for a second."

The axe came back hard against the remaining half of the door a few more times and sent shards of splinters all across the room. I couldn't believe the strength of the young boy when the freshly-removed chunks of the door revealed the kid standing there sucking air with a red face.

Without another word, I rushed hard at the jagged openings in the door and started to push myself through. I quickly felt the boy try and pull me through the chopped wood on the other side and caught my first glimpse of the fire.

A blazing flash of burning red, the fire was flickering from a wing of the house to the left of my door and moving quickly. The tips of the flames were just a few feet away from the boy as he helped me squeeze through the door. I found my footing on the hardwood floor which rested just in front of a flight of steep stairs that descended down into what seemed to be the heart of the old dry house which was starting to burn like a log in a fireplace.

"Downstairs," the young boy yelled in my ear and pulled me towards the stairs just as an amber jumped out of the fire like a flea and singed my shoulder. We rushed down the seemingly endless flight of stairs. I looked up to see an arc of fire crest over the opening at the top of the stairs.

"Oh my God," I screamed.

The fire seemed to move like something out of Fantasia. It flashed down in our direction. We dove to the bottom of the stairs and landed on another hardwood floor. I looked back to see the fire enveloping the stairs we were just on.

We scrambled back to our feet and ran towards an open front door that was just in front of us. I could feel the cold blowing in from the open door and it felt like freedom upon the growing goosebumps on my cold skin.

My eyes soaked in the light of the open door and it almost knocked me over. My eyes hadn't seen pure natural light in months. I had to close them in the pale light of an overcast morning as we ran to the doorway to dull the shine.

I opened my eyes again as I felt us breeze through the open door. My heart sank when my open eyes revealed what was standing on the porch waiting for us.

Carson. Clutching a cold shotgun in the falling rain. The barrel stuck in his mouth. His eyes closed.

My savior stopped abruptly in front of me, slipped on the rain-slicked wood of the deck and fell at Carson's feet.

The shotgun slipped from Carson's grasp and fell to the deck next to the young boy.

I tried to stop myself, but suffered the same fate as the boy and fell hard onto the soggy porch. Carson's fiery eyes locked with mine and went wide.

I turned around to see almost the entire old farmhouse in flames and forgot about Carson for a moment. When I looked back, he was in a wrestling match with the boy for the shotgun.

As you can imagine, the boy didn't stand much of a chance against Carson. It only took a few moments for Carson to wrestle back his weapon. The much larger grown man pulled the shotgun to his shoulder and aimed it right at the boy's forehead.

"No," I screamed, but it was no help.

I closed my eyes and turned away when I heard the blast.

I turned around and thought about running back in the house, but that would be suicide. The fire was now at the foot of the stairs, getting ready to start flickering at my back just outside of the doorway.

No options left, I turned back to the front of the porch where Carson once again had the shotgun shoved in his mouth. He would not be distracted this time though, and I would not turn away.

I watched Carson pull the trigger and watched his headless body tumble to the porch and roll down the stairs until I could no longer see the dark figure.

I had no time to revel in false security. The house was collapsing in ashes behind me and I knew there were numerous potentially-dangerous adults who lived in the house with Carson who could be anywhere right now.

There was something I needed to tend to though before I started to figure out my final escape. I ran over to the young boy's body and knelt down beside him.

He looked up at me, brown eyes welled with tears, and I almost couldn't take it — but held my jaw together tight to keep in the sobs. My movie-trained brain told me I should say things like "You're going to be okay," "You're fine," but I fought back the urge and was relieved to see no blood was coming out of his mouth.

"Are you okay?" I asked.

"I think so," the boy said with pained breaths. "I blocked the gun with my hand. I think it took all of the shot."

The boy lifted a hand that looked fake. His little paw was blown out in the middle of the palm. I could see right through a raggedy hole and see the burning house. I nearly vomited but swallowed down the burning bile back down.

"It's okay, but we gotta get you out of here," I yelled and grabbed hold of the boy's other hand. "Do you know if there are cars with keys in them that run around here or anything?"

The boy winced. He had to be in so much pain.

"I think so. Out by the road. People are always parking their cars there, but we can't let them see us. They will just take us to another house. Maybe even a worse one."

I thought I heard the faint sound of a car whizzing down the highway from off in the distance where tall trees lined the edge of the front yard in front of us.

"Let's go."

I lifted the boy up off the deck, put his weight on my shoulder, and started to descend the slippery stairs with him while also keeping my eyes off of the gory mess that was Carson's body lying at the bottom of the stairs. I never focused in on what was lying there, but based on what I could see out of the corner of my eye, there was no way he was coming back to life.

Our fears rested in what might be waiting for us out by the road.

"The cars will be out there?"

I pointed out in the direction where I thought I heard a car drive by, the edge of the yard, where the tall trees swayed in the wet breeze. The boy barely nodded and I became concerned. He was doing a lot worse than I thought he was at first. I probably didn't consider how much weaker an nine-year-old would be than an adult and he had to of lost a lot of blood already. I was basically lugging him across the wet grass of the yard at this point, he was giving almost nothing and I could carry us both no longer.

We tumbled to the grass in the middle of the yard. I could barely breathe and my muscles ached from just our short journey. I was pretty emaciated after months of being held captive and I barely had any energy or strength.

I wanted to just lay in that soft grass with the cold rain slowly falling on my face forever, but there were two reasons I had to move. The boy's silence, other than for his heavy breathing told me he didn't have long, and I heard the sound of a car pulling onto the gravel road which essentially served as the driveway of the house.

I didn't know exactly what to do though. The grass was long enough to shelter us a bit and we were far enough from the driveway and the house that we would probably only be spotted if someone was really looking for us. Also, getting up and running might actually draw attention to us and give us away.

But I had to make a decision quick. I heard the car engine shut off just in front of the house and allow the crackling of the house fire return to being the loudest sound in my ears.

"Run," the boy whispered at me.

"No."

"Go, to the trees. Once you get there I will scream for help. They will help me. I will be fine and they will be distracted. The cars are on the other side of the trees by the road. It's your best chance. But go, now. Go now. I know who they are. The grandparents. They will take me to the hospital, but they will take you to another house. You have to go now."

I looked over at the boy's eyes one more time. There was something so familiar in them, I felt almost as if I was look into the mirror at my own eyes stuck in a young boy's body.

"What's your name?" I asked.

The boy gulped hard. Maybe blood was starting to come out of his mouth? It took him a while to speak up.

"Scott," he barely got the word out.

"Do you have a full name? I'll look you up if I get away."

"Scott Crestline. Go."

I looked at Scott Crestline for one more second and slipped away.

The run to the trees felt like it took forever, like I was running in slow motion. I felt incredibly vulnerable, waiting for the "grandparents" to shoot me down with Carson's shotgun.

But they didn't. I dove safely into the cover of the trees and the shrubs at their feet. I rested there for a few moments with my eyes glued to the house, the driveway and the yard where the new, young Scott laid. I watched an elderly couple run away from the burning house and towards Scott in the grass before I slipped into the darkness of the tree cover.

I peered at the scene through the bushes and shivered in the cold. The elderly couple knelt down and the man started checking his vitals. The image gave me enough to convince myself that he would be okay and I was coaxed away by the sounds of sirens approaching in the distance.

I quickly discovered Scott had directed me into a mini-forest of sorts. The little patch of tree cover and foliage separated the house's yard from a road for about 25 yards and housed a healthy collection of trash that seemed like it had been tossed out of cars and rusting metal objects. I trudged through a floor of soggy leaves towards a rising embankment and the nearing sounds of sirens.

The embankment was so steep and slick I had to crawl up it on my hands and knees, covering my already dirty sweat pants and sweater in thick mud. I almost slipped and fell back down the thing a few times, but eventually reached the crest where I cautiously peered over the top to lay my eyes upon the true outside world for the first time in quite a while.

Basted in the stale morning light I saw the swift curve of a lonely country road. Lined with moss upon the edges and wet with the rain that had just stopped falling, the road looked like it should be on the cover of some folk rock album. I may have described the setting as beautiful had I not been in the most-perilous situation of my life.

The second thing I noticed was Scott had told me the truth. To my right, the side of the road was lined with cars and camper trailers coated with the green film of algae. I hoped Scott had also told me the truth about some of the vehicles having the keys in them as well. It seemed impossible, but I think I tossed the term impossible out of my mental vocabulary years ago.

My first problem wasn't the keys. It was the approaching sound of sirens roaring up the road to the left. I could not see any emergency vehicles yet, but they were clearly on the way and they kept me tucked behind the brim of the embankment, hoping to not be spotted. Right now, I figured not getting involved in what I imagined was some kind of podunk town law enforcement or fire department probably made up of people who kept me captured in the house was not a good idea. I needed to just get the fuck out of this place on my own until I found civilization and then give Oprah a call. This was on me now. I couldn't rely on anyone else for a while.

I finally saw a red fire truck become a dot on my left horizon. The piercing sound of the roaring siren pierced my ears until I saw the hefty thing slow to nearly a stop to conquer the heavy curve just in front of me.

I congratulated myself for the decision not to flag the thing down when I saw it pass and laid eyes upon the burly mountain men who clung to the thing in tattered firefighter gear. I got a second positive confirmation when a sheriff's car whipped by behind the fire truck commanded by a guy in aviators sporting a handlebar mustache.

I watched the vehicles fade from my sight to the right. I pulled myself up onto the side of the road behind the final car in the line that snaked next to the edge of the pavement.

The car at the back of the line looked like something a pimp would drive in a 70s cop movie. Deep purple with gold accents and blocky, the thing was coated with moss and I don't know how it could run. I passed it up for the next option, which was an only slightly-newer little hatchback.

The door to the little red hatchback gave a slight fight when I tried to open it, but eventually gave out and released an almost overwhelming smell of mildew which wafted into my open mouth. I held my breath and ducked into the darkened interior of the thing which smelled like an ancient fart.

I had no time to focus on the stomach-turning smell. I

heard the sound of a car cutting the wind behind me rolling down the road and ducked below the vantage point of my new car's windows and windshield until I heard the car whoosh past me.

Once in the clear I searched the interior of the car for any signs of a key. The center console, the glove compartment, underneath the rug mats, underneath the seats. I found a wealth of cigarette butts, dried-out lipsticks and gum wrappers but no keys. I let out a deep exhale behind the wheel and dreaded sneaking back out into the vulnerable cold, knowing that enough time had passed to where my living captors were probably starting to look for me. I had to move fast.

I grabbed hold of the door handle and readied to exit when the glint of something shiny caught the corner of my eye.

The keys were dangling down from the ignition.

Oh my God.

I frantically scrambled with the keys before cranking them with an anxious prayer for a start repeating in my head.

Please God start. Please God start. Please God start.

The engine started. Maybe my horror movie was coming to a close? The entire car rumbled and I gave it a little while to warm up while another car whooshed by. I prayed they didn't see me as I didn't have time to duck down and hide.

It had been so long since I had driven a car, the whole experience seemed alien to me. I clumsily executed a three-point turn in the middle of the road, hoping no one would come until I was backing up just a little bit to give myself the last inches I needed to accelerate into freedom.

I let out a painful exhale and flicked on the heat. The first flicker of even just lukewarm air pushing out the vents soothed my soul, but it was just a momentary massage.

Another car passed me going the other direction on the road just as I eased onto the gas. Piloted by a middle-aged couple with weathered faces and fresh cigarettes, their eyes glued to me until our gazes faded and I drove around the corner.

10

Sometime That Night

I don't know how long I had drove. No idea what day it was. No idea what the exact time was. The clock in the car read 3:30 a.m. but that couldn't have been the time. I wasn't exactly sure what time of year it was, Winter maybe? There were hints of old snow on the ground. All I knew was I had driven that filthy hatchback straight without a single stop until the sun had set for quite a while and its fuel gauge neared empty.

I had no idea where I was. I simply followed the road I started on until I reached a poor excuse for a town and went in any direction I could from there on out that seemed like it had the best chance at eventually reaching some kind of acceptable civilization. I hadn't found luck with that just yet, but I did reach an officially tagged Washington state highway just before sunset and had been following it for a couple of hours now. Signs had been marking a city I had heard of before called Spokane for a while now, but it was still triple digits away at this point and I had no choice but to stop when the fuel gauge dipped to empty.

The only gas station I had seen since that first town was just a way back on the road so I figured my safest bet was to double back and fill up there and access my overall situation as well. I passed up the station the first time around because a cluster of bikers were posted up in front of it, but I no longer had that kind of flexibility. There was no telling how far the next gas station could be and how reliable the fuel gauge in the car even was, so I turned back around on the dark highway.

I made it back to the gas station and it lonely single streetlamp that illuminated two fuel pumps and a three-spot parking lot in front of a mini-mart-style building about the size of a one-bedroom apartment. I pulled up to one of the pumps and was relieved to see lights on inside the mart and a buzzing neon OPEN sign in the door window.

A realization came over me when I walked from the car to the mart. I had no money, no credit or debit cards, no identification. All I had were the filthy clothes upon my body, a car that may have been reported as stolen and whatever the hell was in it.

I hadn't seen any money when I searched the car. I thought I may have seen a book of checks, but shit, I don't think even a gas station like this in the middle of nowhere would take a check, let alone one without ID. It was time. It was time for me to pack it in, tell the person behind the counter my story and wait for some kind of authorities to show up and hope they believed my story. I was at least three hours or so away from the house where I had been held captive. There was no chance there was some grander conspiracy at hand that could do me in at this point.

The relief of my decision gave me a high. I felt as if I was walking on air when I stepped up to the mart door until I tried to push the thing open and it wouldn't budge.

"What the hell?" I screeched, drawing the attention of an old codger behind the counter, distracting him from the soft sound of a baseball game on the radio and something he was doing that required a lot of receipts being spread out across the counter.

"We're closed," he announced without even looking at me for more than half a second before putting his glasses back on the receipts.

I pounded on the glass of the door as hard as I could, not even caring if I broke the fucking thing.

"No, no, no. I need help," I yelled.

The old man didn't look at me, just kept examining the receipts.

"We close at eight. The sign right in front of you says that. No exceptions. I already closed the register so I can't even sell you anything, ma'am."

"Fuck you. I just need to use your phone," I yelled.

The old man gathered up his receipts in a sweep and started to walk away from the counter.

"There's a payphone out front. And, yes, it works. I'm done doing any business with you lady," he said and disappeared from sight.

I was enraged, but happy to hear about the payphone. I was sure you could call 911 for free on those things. Knowing the end of my journey was now just a phone call away, that sense of relief came right back.

Until I turned around and saw a familiar-looking car parked next to mine at the pump. It was dated, bulky, purple and its gold accents shimmered in the street lamp before it shut off in unison with the light inside the mart and my world fell into darkness.

11

In the Cold Darkness

I stayed with my back glued to the glass entry door of the mart, unable to move. I couldn't see anyone in the car, whoever was driving was somewhere on the property, but I had yet to see a sign of them. All I could sense was the stinging cold, bitter wind and misleading darkness.

My eyes fluttered around the parking lot, but even they were so tired I almost didn't trust them anymore. Like an injured gazelle pursued by lions for days, I was just about ready to throw in the towel and just give up.

But a ray of hope shot through me when I had a realization. The purple car was running, no one was behind the wheel.

I took off in an exhausted sprint towards the car. The volume of its rumbling engine picked up with every step until I was at the driver's side door.

I threw myself behind the wheel, slammed down the mechanical lock next to me. I ripped the gear into drive as swiftly as I could and almost cried when I started to idle the car towards the highway.

This was finally my moment. I had the keys to the other car in my pocket, there was no way whoever was hiding back at the station had a way to follow me in a vehicle.

My breaths were rushed and ragged, my wheezes provided

the haggard soundtrack as I raced up the highway back in the direction that should have led towards civilization.

I caught my breath quicker than I thought I would, but even with lungs filled with oxygen, I could still hear the sound of heavy breathing.

I looked in the rear view mirror and saw a figure sitting up in the backseat. I couldn't make out their face or appearance at all, just could see they were wearing a sleep apnea mask before the car flew off the highway and I shut my eyes and braced for the crash.

12

Awake

God damn it was cold.

That was my first waking thought, before I even opened my eyes. I just felt myself wrapped up in the frigid cold. My body was on the verge of shivering.

I opened my eyes to see a world of white. An overall sense of nothingness and a clean palate fell upon me before the objects in my fresh new world began to take shape.

I tried to move, couldn't. My eyes finally fully focused to reveal my bruised arms strapped to a bed of thin white linens. I struggled again, no luck, my lashings were much too tight for my withered body to struggle against.

I screamed, but my cry was muffled. My face was strapped as well, lashed with the thick plastic of a sleep apnea mask. Its mechanical whizz and whines filled my ears with a numbing, repetitive score.

What I was hearing wasn't just the sound of my mask though. I wiggled up in my bed just a little bit to scan the drafty room. I was resting in an expansive hospital room in the middle of a thick sea of other beds, all lashed with bodies dressed in drab hospital gowns connected to sleep apnea machines ringing out into the cold room. Their machines whined into the air like some kind of morbid orchestra.

I closed my eyes and listened to the machines rise and fall, staring at the darkness of my mind. My initial urge was to try and fight, try and escape, but the great fatigue of my mind and body didn't let those thoughts sprout legs this time.

It was okay. It was all going to be okay.

Sleep would come soon enough.

Thought Catalog, it's a website.
www.thoughtcatalog.com

Social
facebook.com/thoughtcatalog
twitter.com/thoughtcatalog
tumblr.com/thoughtcatalog
instagram.com/thoughtcatalog

Corporate
www.thought.is

About the Author

A lifelong writer, Jack grew up in the woods of Washington, where he started his horror writing career in the second grade when he put out his own scary story books and sold them to classmates. Since then, Jack has written professionally as a journalist, fiction writer and ghost writer with his work being featured in publications such as ESPN, *Men's Fitness*, Thought Catalog/Creepy Catalog, *The Los Angeles Times*, *The Seattle Times* and many other popular publications. His horror writing on Creepy Catalog has been particularly popular and has led to him being hired as a featured writer for the site.

Jack moved to Los Angeles after graduating with a journalism degree from Washington State University and resides in the Hollywood area with his wife Caitlin.

www.ingramcontent.com/pod-product-compliance
Lightning Source LLC
Chambersburg PA
CBHW032108170626
46808CB00008B/2985